Kids Living Green

Let's Save Water!

by Jenna Lee Gleisner

Bullfrog Books

Ideas for Parents and Teachers

Bullfrog Books let children practice reading informational text at the earliest reading levels. Repetition, familiar words, and photo labels support early readers.

Before Reading
- Discuss the cover photo. What does it tell them?
- Look at the picture glossary together. Read and discuss the words.

Read the Book
- "Walk" through the book and look at the photos. Let the child ask questions. Point out the photo labels.
- Read the book to the child, or have him or her read independently.

After Reading
- Prompt the child to think more. Ask: Saving fresh water and using it wisely is important. How do you help save water every day?

Bullfrog Books are published by Jump!
5357 Penn Avenue South
Minneapolis, MN 55419
www.jumplibrary.com

Library of Congress Cataloging-in-Publication Data is available at www.loc.gov or upon request from the publisher.

ISBN: 978-1-64128-459-2 (hardcover)
ISBN: 978-1-64128-460-8 (paperback)
ISBN: 978-1-64128-461-5 (ebook)

Editor: Susanne Bushman
Designer: Molly Ballanger

Photo Credits: Dave_Pot/iStock, cover; MAHATHIR MOHD YASIN/Shutterstock, 1; Nikitin Victor/Shutterstock, 3; Greta Nurk/ Shutterstock, 4; EpicStockMedia/Shutterstock, 5, 23bl; Wavebreakmedia/iStock, 6–7; vasiliki/ Getty, 8–9; Littlekidmoment/Shutterstock, 10, 11; THEPALMER/iStock, 12–13 (foreground); David Gilder/Shutterstock, 12–13 (background); Sam Bloomberg-Rissman/Blend Images/Superstock, 14–15; Igor Pushkarev/Shutterstock, 16; ConstantinosZ/Shutterstock, 17 (hand); Piotr Piatrouski/Shutterstock, 17 (ice cube); shyya/Shutterstock, 17 (plant); Blend Images - KidStock/Getty, 18–19, 23tr; Blend Images/ Superstock, 20–21; Chonlawut/Shutterstock, 22; zhangyang13576997233/Shutterstock, 23tl; Andrea Izzotti/Shutterstock, 23br; Jim Barber/Shutterstock, 24.

Printed in the United States of America at Corporate Graphics in North Mankato, Minnesota.

Table of Contents

Use Less

Let's save water!
Why?

Most of Earth's water is in oceans.

It has salt.

We have to treat it.

This uses energy.

Then we can drink it.

There is only so much
fresh water.

We can save it every day.

How?

Jon turns off the water.

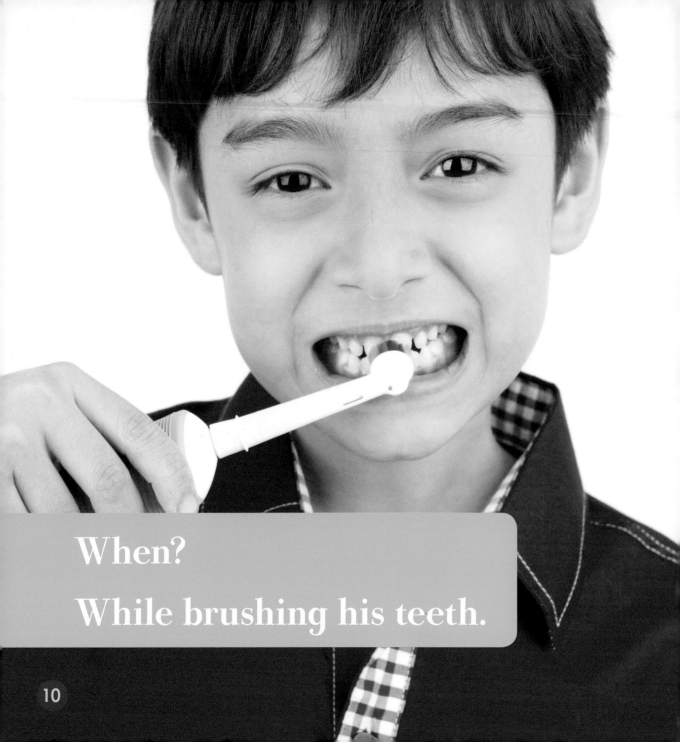

When?

While brushing his teeth.

And while washing
his hands.

11

Bo washes his dog.

He fills a bucket.

He turns the hose off.

This uses less water.

hose

bucket

13

Rae fills the washer full.
Why?
So she doesn't have
to run it as often.

Min doesn't drink all of her water.

She waters plants with it.

16

ice cube

She waters with ice cubes, too!

17

This faucet dripped.

We fixed it!

This saves water, too.

faucet

Can you save water?
Yes!
How will you do it?

Let's Do It!

Collect Rainwater

Another way to save water is to collect it! Does your house have gutters? Put a pail or barrel below them to catch rainwater that runs off the roof.

Be sure to check laws in your area. Some places have laws about how much water you can collect.

You can then use the collected water to water your garden or plants. Or to wash your bike or a car. What other ways could you use your collected rainwater?

Picture Glossary

energy
Power from coal, electricity, or other sources that makes machines work and produces heat.

faucet
A device with a valve that turns the flow of water on or off.

oceans
The bodies of salt water that cover nearly three fourths of the Earth's surface.

treat
To clean or change. Salt water is treated at a plant to remove the salt so we can drink it.

Index

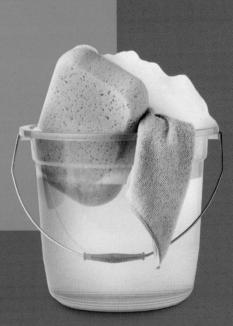

To Learn More

Finding more information is as easy as 1, 2, 3.

❶ Go to www.factsurfer.com

❷ Enter "let'ssavewater!" into the search box.

❸ Click the "Surf" button to see a list of websites.

24